Alpha's Rejected Mate

by

(Christina Castillo)

Table of Contents

The Beginning

Before I tell you my story, let me start from the beginning. Many moons ago, werewolves existed. There was a beautiful woman named Selene. She had a devoted and loving husband. He built her a house in the woods, away from people. Selene didn't mind since she was an animal lover. She had always loved the wilderness. She always attracts the critters, and she seems to be able to talk to them. In those days, she would have been killed and called a witch. Her husband believe that God did not make mistakes.

One night there was a stranger passing through. Selene and her husband fed him and let him spend the night. Selene made a bed in the barn for him to sleep. He was to leave in the morning after he got a good night's sleep. The stranger grabbed her by the hair and said, "You are mine now." He was forcing himself on her. He managed to rip her clothes off. There was a pack of wolves passing by. They attacked the man, killing him. Selene was so heartbroken seeing her dead husband. She went inside to put clothes on.

He stabbed him in the back. When her husband fell, he stabbed his heart. Selene felt her husband was taking too long. She decided to go look for him. When she went outside, she saw he husband bleeding out. Selene started to run to him. The stranger grabs her by the hair and says you are mine now." He was forcing himself on her. He managed to rip her clothes off. There was a pack of wolves passing by. They attacked the man killing him. Selene was so heartbroken seeing her dead husband. She went inside to put clothes on.

The woman, in her grief, did not fear the wolves. She started to dig a grave for her husband. One of the wolves was watching from afar. When she finished digging the grave, she went into the house to get water. When she came outside, she saw the wolves pulling the man towards the grave.

They let him fall into the grave. She was surprised but was not afraid. She went out and started to cover him with the dirt. The wolves helped her bury her husband. In gratitude, she made a stew and shared it with the wolves. She knew her husband was too heavy for her to put him in the grave. The wolves started to hunt and bring her rabbits, a boar, and deer for her. She would skin and clean the animal. She would either dry the meat for it not to spoil. She would also make stews and share them with the wolves. She started selling skins in town to buy other essentials such as flour, sugar, and coffee. She would buy things to make her own soaps. She started to sell those in town, also.

As time passes by, she is lonely and desires to have a husband. She was very close to the Alpha of the Pack. Every night she would look into the sky, asking God for a new husband. She wished the wolf could be a man to help her. The wolf would look into the moon and ask for her to be a wolf.

On the next full moon, he heard a voice telling him to bite the woman on the shoulder. The woman was lying on the ground, looking at the stars. He went up to her and bit her. The woman screams in pain when she begins to shift into a silver wolf. They were happy and started to hunt and play as pups. When they were tired, they fell asleep. The woman woke a human again. There was a naked man next to her. She recognized his eye and realized it was the wolf.

The Pack of wolves started to shift into humans. The men were tall and muscular to be able to protect the Pack. That is when the first werewolves were formed. The wolfs still have the same laws as the Pack. When they find their mate, they mate for life. As a symbol of the first werewolf, they mark their mates. It solidifies their bond.

One night a stranger came a calling. He looked off, and he wanted Selene as his bride. He snuck up behind her and tried to steal her. She managed to fight him off and ran to her mate. When she looks back, she steps in front of an arrow meant for her husband. Before she died, she cursed the man. "I Selene luna of my pack. Curse you to walk the night and burn from the sun since you used a wooden arrow. You will die of a wooded stake or arrow through your heart. I curse you not to know what love feels until you change. Since you spilled my blood, you will only crave blood to live. The food you eat will rot in your mouth".

The man became pale, and fangs began to form. He took off running into the night. That is how the vampires were born and enemies of the werewolves. She promised to give every wolf a mate. They will find each other from a scent that only they can smell. With a touch, you will feel the sparks go through your body. The mates will feel each other's emotions and speak telepathically. The Alpha will make others into werewolves to form a larger pack for protection. Selene took her last breath and floated to the moon. She became the Moon Goddess, the goddess of the werewolves.

Demetria Dennison

My name is Demetria Dennison (aka Demi). I am a Warrior in training. I get a lot of teasing since I am a runt. I am 5' tall compared to normal she-wolves; they are usually '5'7' and over. My pack name is the Red Moon Pack. We have a total of 250 members, not including the pups. We have a lake and a forest surrounding us. We have our own little town. We have humans that drive throughout town, so we have to be careful about shifting into our wolf.

My mother is the first in command of the warriors. My mother, Donna Dennison, trains the adult warriors. If there is a war or an attack, she leads them. She is a war strategist and a weapons specialist. She is feared for her fighting skills. She has a duo placement in the Pack. She is also a skilled tracker and scout. Mom had trained since a pup from both of her parents. Many werewolves are scared of here and don't mess with our Pack.

My dad is a Beta (second in command) at the Blue Moon Pack. I face time with dad all the time. I spend most weekends and some holidays with him. My dad and mom are not fated mates but love each other fiercely. Their fated mates died in a war before I was born. They are high-ranking wolves in different packs. Marking each other will make it difficult to be separated from each other. Marking is when two mates bite each other's shoulders to show they belong together. It keeps others away from them. Werewolves are possessive over their mates.

My parents stay connected by face timing every day. When they are off duty, they are together. They have a very loyal and monogamous relationship with each other. On their days off, they will be at each other's packs. We go on family vacations once a year. Hey, if it works for them, who am I to judge? I am close to both of my parents, but I live with my mom. I have a room in the pack house for when Mom goes on missions. The Alpha and Luna treat me like their daughter, and if needed, they reprimand me.

Mom is best friends with Luna Alicia. My mom is Alpha's favorite high-ranking werewolf. I am staying in the pack house this week since mom is on a mission. I am getting ready for school, and I hear my best friend Louie (aka Lucy Lue) singing Happy Birthday. She walks in with a triple chocolate cupcake with a single candle on it. I can smell the sweetness of the buttercream frosting. It makes my mouth water. I have a sweet tooth, and chocolate is my kryptonite. I smile, making a wish before blowing out the candle. I grab my keys and tell her, 'Let's go; Beasty is waiting." I have a purple convertible, a 69 SS Camaro, that my dad bought and restored for me. He custom-painted it with my favorite color, purple. It has hot pink racing stripes over the hood to the back of the spoiler. I have hot pink seats with everything else black. I named it beasty for the sound of the engine. (It has a four-barrel 350 engine)

Today I turned seventeen and could find my mate today. Some wolves do not find their other half for years. Every year a different pack will throw the mate gala. This year it is our Pack throwing the gala. It will be held in our ballroom. If you have not found your mate by chance, you will be there. We arrive at school, and we see the future Alpha Justin Thomas. Justin and I recognize each other as mates. He rushed to me and kissed me softly, saying, "MATE."

Justin came to my room after school. He wants to mark and fully mate with me. Fully mated is when we mark each other while having sex. We begin to kiss, and before I know it, we are on the bed. I gave my virginity to my mate. When we finished, I realized I was not marked. I looked at Justin, confused, and he gave me an evil smirk. Justin is now above me, smirking, ready to break my heart.

I hear the worst words a mate can tell you. "I, Justin Thomas, future alpha of the Red Moon Pack, reject you, Demetria Dennison, as my mate and future Luna." I got what I wanted, and thank you. The pain I felt was unbearable as my heart shattered to pieces. I watch him get dressed before walking out. I just lay there in shock and not believing what just happened. How could he do this to me? We grew up together as good friends. He once told me he hoped we were mates. Is this why he wanted to be my mate? He wanted to be my mate to hurt me. Not in my wildest dreams did I see this coming.

Louie came looking for me when I did not go down for dinner. I am crying uncontrollably as she runs to comfort me. I told her what happened. Suddenly I felt extreme pain in my stomach, thighs, breast, arms, and bruises were forming in those areas. Then everything turns black. I wake with Louie holding my hand.

The Alpha and Luna came running to see what was going on. Luna Alicia heard that the doctor had been called to my room. Suddenly the door swings open, and Justin walks in with fury in his eyes. He yells, "OUT OF JEALOUSY, YOU KILLED MARY FINN"! I looked at him and said, "That was who you were with"? Is this what you wanted? I swung open my robe. He looks at me in shock and regret. I am standing there in my bra and underwear, not caring about the crowd at my door. His dad stands up and asks him, "You did this to your mate."

Then my wolf (Nyx) comes forward, stands on a table, and remembers I am a runt. She grabs Justin by the neck and yells through growls. My human, your rejected mate, has not left this room since you rejected her, jackass. I do not know who killed your power-hungry slut. I hope the sloppy thirds were worth hurting your mate. She screwed both your Gamma and Beta before you. Who knows with who else she had sex?

Nyx throws him across the room and gives me control back. I walk to him and yell, "I, DEMETTIA DENNISON, ACCEPT YOUR REJECTION AS YOU MATE AND FUTURE LUNA OF THE RED MOON PACK. NOW GET THE HELL OUT OF MY ROOM, NOW!" I yelled with all my might and my beta/alpha blood aura coming through. With that, he got up and ran past the crowd that was in the hall. I walked over and slammed the door shut.

I asked the Alpha if I could have permission to temporarily move with my dad. I want to heal my heart, and that will be hard seeing Justin every day. He rubs my back, saying I will call Alpha Red. He says start packing, sweetheart. Luna Alicia says promise me you will call me every day. I promised her that I would; I saw Louie crying uncontrollably, and I went to hug her. I will come back, I honestly promised her. We will face time every day.

I had to wait for mom to come back. Without her, I cannot complete the final papers needed for the transfer. I also had to have mom sign papers to transfer schools. Justin would follow me for two weeks at school. I would see him staring at me during training. It is so creepy the way he became my stalker. I am happy he has not tried to talk to me. I do not know how I would react if he got near me.

I loaded up my car and said my goodbyes. I have a lot of friends that were outside giving me hugs and gifts. I felt like someone was watching me. I looked to the side of the house, and there was Justin. He had regret and sadness in his eyes. I ignored him and finished my goodbyes.

The Blue Moon Pack

It has been two weeks now, and I am at my dad's Pack. I arrived at the Blue Moon Pack, and my dad was waiting outside the front door. We both ran to each other with arms wide open, and he spun me around. I could feel his happiness through his laughter. "Dad, I am not a little girl anymore," I say. He laughs and says, "But you will always be my little warrior."

I am a runt in the Pack, so my height is always brought up. He tells the omega to take my bags to my room. He walks me to Alpha Red's office. His real name is Donny O'Hara. He has intense red hair, so everyone calls him Red. His office has a masculine feel to it, with black couches and a table. There's a dart game on one wall and bookshelves made of mahogany wood, complete with matching coffee and end tables.

I walk in, and he comes and gives me a hug. He asks, "So, little one, tell me what happened that you needed an escape?" It was more of a command than a question. I tell him everything that happened with tears in my eyes, and I see dad trying to control his wolf. Red says, "That little ass is going to painfully hear from me. How dare he reject our little warrior. Doesn't he know we can snap his neck like a twig?" I giggle, telling the guys to leave him alone. "My wolf will take care of him when my heart is healed."

Suddenly, Dad jumps up and says, "Red, do you hear or smell that? It is faint, but it is there." Alphas have better noses than the average wolf. They can smell a she-wolf pregnant, even if it is a few days. My father has alpha blood, so his nose is just as strong. My dad's eyes open wide, and he says, "Our baby is pregnant." I said, "Huh, no way! I was not in heat." He says, "Alpha blooded wolves do not have to be in heat to get pregnant. Baby, you have alpha blood. You had sex for the first time with your alpha mate." I say, "Holy shit, wait until I see him. I am going to kick his ass."

Suddenly, it kicks in. I whisper, "I am pregnant. What the hell am I going to do now?" I start to panic and pace the room. Both men watch as I pace, and my dad says, "Little warrior, we will help you." I am walking in a daze back to my room. I decide to FaceTime with mom, crying. I told her what dad and Alpha Red told me. She was ecstatic to be a grandma, and then Alicia walked in. She sees me on the phone crying and asks, "What is wrong, baby?" I told her that dad could smell me pregnant. I beg them, "Please leave this between us." Of course, I know Alicia was going to tell Mark. Justin rejected me two weeks ago, so that means he rejected my baby. Wolf laws state he has no right to my baby, I state to the two women. The luna looks sad but says that the law also states: "Firstborn is still the future Alpha." It does not matter if he has other children. I had no idea of that part of the law.

Angry Dads

I started reacquainting with my friends from this Pack. I was starting to feel happy and more like myself. I was challenged by one of the warriors in training. She wanted a friendly fight in human form. I accepted, and we went at it. I was winning our sparring match when we heard a loud growl. We looked over and saw Alpha Red. He yells, "DEMETRIA DENNISON, GET YOUR BUTT OUT OF THAT RING NOW!" with a loud growl. Wow, he used my full name. That is a first; he might be really pissed off. Everyone around us bowed submissively. I have alpha blood, so it does not always affect me the same way.

Today I was submissive with all his power radiating off him. I jumped out, and he yelled, "MY OFFICE NOW!" I walked with my head down, knowing I was in trouble. I felt like a little girl being sent to my room. I can hear Red mumbling, "What the hell was she thinking fighting in her condition." The Alpha is growling, and dad is not far behind us doing the same thing. I can hear Nyx in my head laughing at me; I tell her to shut up. Nyx is singing, "You are in trouble and being sent to the principal's office." I snap at her, saying, "Shut up, Nyx!" She is laughing in my head. Nyx, that means you cannot fight either; that is when she stops laughing. She says, "What the hell, dammit? I am going to kick our mate's ass." He is not our mate, I say angrily at Nyx. "You have to wait until after the baby is born; remember, we are in trouble for sparring."

Alpha Red scolds me because I am not supposed to be fighting. Dad is right there with him, making me feel ganged up on. I said if I do not get hit in the stomach, the exercise is good for me. I see him mind-linking someone, and the door opens a few minutes later. The doctor walks in and says, "Yes, Alpha, how can I help you?" My mouth falls open while dropping my head into my hands. I cannot believe he called the doctor; how embarrassing. I skipped our appointment, not ready to accept that I was pregnant.

He asks the doctor if I should be training in the ring. She shakes her head no, saying, "No, Alpha. She could be hit in the wrong place or shift. She can do simple human exercises like yoga, pilates, and walking on the treadmill. She can take nature walks, which I recommend. It will help with her delivery. Demi always needs to keep hydrated. She should eat four meals a day with snacks in between. If she had kept her appointment, I would have told her all of this." I hear Nyx calling her a narc. "Here are the vitamins she needs to take daily. If morning sickness affects her, she needs to eat broth and saltine crackers. She cannot shift either because this can abort the baby." He says, "Thank you, doctor." The doctor looks at me and says, "When you are finished here, please come to my office." She closes the door softly when she walks out.

They take turns scolding me again. I hate it when I have two father figures in the same place. They scolded me for thirty minutes. They were angry now for skipping my appointment. They tell me how important the Dr. visits are, and I have to keep them. Red even mentioned if I miss another appointment, he will personally take me. Dad then tells me, "Now go see the doctor." I am looking at them, and I say, "Yes, sirs" and salute. They burst out laughing while shaking their heads.

I walk into the doctor's office, and she does a full checkup. After the blood and urine test, she gives me an ultrasound. The doctor tells me I look healthy, and my baby is growing normally. She says it is too soon to find out the sex. "Here is your appointment card. Next time, we can do another ultrasound." The doctor says, "I was commanded to inform the Alpha if you miss another visit."

Great, when an alpha commands you, you cannot disobey him.

When I walked out of one of the clinics, my friend Luke Logan saw me in tears. He says, "Come walk with me." We start walking a path that leads to a private garden. I look around and say, "This is beautiful." Luke looks into my eyes and asks, "What is wrong?" I was hesitant to say anything. I ask him, "Whether I am appealing to guys?" He smiles and asks, "What kind of question is that? You are a beautiful, kind, charismatic girl, and you have a badass car." I burst out laughing while blushing.

I say, "Hey, let us get a burger in town. I will give you a ride in my beasty." He says, "Let us go." I mind link dad, telling him where we are going. He answers, "OK" and asks if it is a craving. I just laughed and told him I would be back soon. I got my keys and met Luke outside. We arrive at the diner, and we tell the waitress our order. I got a mind link from dad asking me to bring him a double cheeseburger combo with an extra order of onion rings. He tells me to put our orders on his account. He says that he already mind-linked the manager. Then Red links me, saying, "Baby, please double your dad's order. Thank you. Love you, baby." I tell Luke, "Do not let me forget my dad's orders. I am already in hot water with them."

Top of Form

Lukes Promise

Luke asks, "Are you going to tell me what is wrong?" I tell him everything my mate did. He looks angry with his fist in a tight ball. I tell him how he rejected me and accused me of killing his slut. I finish off with how my dad tag-teamed while scolding me. Then Alpha Red links the doctor, and she kind of scolded me too. "I am at least lucky I have my dad helping me out," I say.

"I promise I will be there for you too," says Luke. True to his promise, Luke was there for every craving, every discomfort, and every mood swing for four months. Luke was caught in my mood swings, and dad felt sorry for him. Dad teases that he sometimes acts like he is the father of the baby. I have to admit I liked the way he treated me. I know he is not my mate, but I do appreciate him. He has been a godsend.

I went into labor, and my two dads and Luke were there with me. Five hours later, my son, Zander Thomas, was born. I gave him his dad's surname because his grandparents asked me to. I will do anything for them. They are second parents to me. They always treated me and mom as family.

Zander Thomas

Zander is a happy baby; he loves to giggle and play with my hair. The first month was hard with the lack of sleep and his colic. I barely got any rest. My dads were overjoyed with him and were making plans to raise him as a strong warrior. Mom and Alicia made a trip to visit us. They were spoiling him every chance they got.

Where has the time gone? Zander is now eight months old; he is trying to walk now. Zander is alert to his surroundings now. He still likes playing with my hair when I hold him. I wonder if that is normal. I make his baby food homemade. I puree fresh vegetables and fruits. I also puree chicken and beef for him to get healthy meals without preservatives. He is a good eater and has gained his normal weight. He is a very active boy, and now he is walking. I am getting my exercise chasing him around.

I just got mind-linked from my dad. He wants me to join him in the Alpha's office. I walk in, and I see dad in tears, saying, "Your mom was hurt." I run to his side to understand him better. It is hard to hear the words between his sobbing.

"Six Rogues ambushed her, and she needs to talk to you. She is in bad shape and is asking for you," dad says. "Tell your mom I love her, and I will see her tonight. Come with me, please, dad," I say. He replies, "Go ahead; I will be right behind you." I nod, and I ask, "How bad is mom? I fear what I will find when I arrive." Dad never cries, so this must be serious. He has always been the level-headed person, not showing his emotions in disasters.

Going Home

I pack our bags with a stroller. I decided to buy a playpen there because it does not fit in my Beasty. I looked at dad, and he said, "Tell your mom I love her." I say ok and give him hugs and kisses. I am worried because dad kept telling me to tell mom he loved her. It made me feel something bad was going to happen.

I drive to my old Pack in deep thought. I had to make a few stops to change diapers or feed Zander. I stopped at Walmart when I was almost there to buy a playpen. I tied it to the roof since I am close to the Pack. I finally made it there, and Louie was outside waiting for me. She says, "Come on, I will show you where she is." I hand the keys to one of the omegas to unload the car. I inform them to take it to mom's house.

I walked in, and the first pup I saw was Alpha Justin. His eyes widened upon seeing

Zander. I kept walking to the hospital and saw my mom on machines. I started to tear up and ran to her bed. She sees Zander smiling lovingly at us. She says, "Let me see my precious pup." She sheds some tears, holding my pup tight to her chest. He is giggling while playing with her necklace. She takes in his scent, saying, "I love the scent of pups. Especially my big boy here," she tells him. I tell her dad was coming, and he sent his love. She giggles, saying, "I love that man with all my heart."

"Baby," she says, "I have a large amount of silver and wolfbane in me. A witch cursed me so I could be taken down. The crap just hit the ceiling; I could not believe my ears. 'I am dying. My wolf is already dead,' mom says. Talk about being blunt and straight to the point. 'I do not know how much time I have. I want you to know I have made a will. You and the baby have a large amount of money and a home. Your dad will also receive a business he helped me start in the city. You will never need anything from a man if that is what you wish. Promise me you will not give up on love not every man is Justin. Who knows, you might meet your second chance, mate'? I cried when she kissed me on my forehead. I am in a daze trying to absorb everything I just heard. Dad came running in, asking if I made it. I nodded and decided to give them a minute. Dad links me to come back in. I pick up Zander from mom's lap. Suddenly, she looks at us with love and gasps. Then she was gone. I yell, "Mom, come back. I need you." I am shaking her to see, not believing I lost her. I hear the sad howls around the Pack as they disconnect from mom. When a wolf with high status dies, the Pack will feel the disconnection. They know mom has died and are heartbroken. Mom was loved by the whole Pack.

I walked out crying uncontrollably. I handed Zander to Louie. "Please watch him and me shift midair, running, howling in pain." After about an hour, I decided to go back and check on my son. As soon as I walked into the packhouse, I felt myself shoved up against the wall. Justin says through gritted teeth, "You kept my son from me." I grabbed his hand and twisted it from my neck, breaking it. I say, "No, Zander Thomas is my son."

"The day we found out we were mates, you rejected me and our bond. You got what you wanted and left me, so back off. We heard loud gasps and growls in the room we were in. You have no claim over Zander Thomas by wolf law. You reject your mate. You are rejecting your kids. According to wolf law, it does not matter if you have other kids. Zander is the future Alpha of the Red Moon Pack. Now excuse me. I have a funeral to arrange."

I walked away to my mom's cottage. Mom's omega was already unpacking for me. She was in tears, and I had to hug her. She was mom's personal omega for many years. She used to take care of me when I was growing up. Mom left her some money in the will for her loyalty. Mom paid her better than other high-ranking pack members.

The next day, we are preparing for the funeral of the Head Warrior, aka my mother.

The Alpha and Luna shared wonderful memories of my mom. Many warriors and guards had good stories about my mom. Alpha Red and my dad went on the stage next and talked about mom. They have some funny stories too.

Dad admitted mom kicked his ass the first time they met. He fell in love with her that instant. She was the most beautiful woman he had ever met. He laughs, saying she made me work to win her over. It was the best thing I ever did in my life, dad says with tears falling. She became the love of my life, and I will miss her.

I walked up there, and I couldn't talk. Every time I tried to speak, nothing would come out. I burst into tears, and dad had to help me walk away. Zander was in tears, not knowing what was going on. I believe he could feel the sadness in the Pack.

We all walked to the cemetery where my mother was buried. I will never have late-night talks or movie marathons while eating junk food. Zander will never know my mom growing up. I am crying so loud until I pass out. I woke up in my mom's house. Dad told me he had to go back home. He had pack business to finish. I knew he was going to throw himself into work.

I had to stay a week or so to pack mom's things. I packed what I wanted and gave away the rest. Some of it I left for mom's omega. I told mom's omega I was going to leave her mom's house. She was a single mom and lived in a rundown shack. All her money went to her kids. Her mate was killed when a rogue attacked the

Pack. She hugged me and thanked me. She still was not able to talk about her mom. She was heartbroken, as we were.

The lawyer came and had me sign some papers. I was surprised at what mom had done financially. I asked him to draw up a paper to transfer the house to mom's omega. He agreed and told me he would call me when it was done. I showed him to the door, and we said our goodbyes.

There was a knock on the door, and it was Justin. I ask what the hell do you want? He asks, "Can I see my son, please?" I tell him, "You mean my son?" He nods. "Please, you are leaving tomorrow, and I will not see him anymore." I hesitated but gave in. He runs out of the house with Zander in his arms. There were guards blocking my way out. He said, "Sorry, the Alpha does not want you to leave your house."

I mind-link Alpha Mark and tell him that Justin took Zander. The guards will not let me out of mom's house. I cry to the Alpha. I look at the guards, and I can tell that they have got a mind link. They move aside for me, and I take off running. I was following my son's scent. I found Justin in the living room playing with Zander. I go to get Zander, and Justin keeps giving me his back. I am in tears begging for him to give me Zander. We hear a loud growl, and we look at the direction it came from.

Alpha Mark commands Justin to give me my baby back. He walks up to Justin and punches him. "Son, you are not fit to be an Alpha. I am not retiring anytime soon, so you better grow up. You have broken wolf law," he turns to look at me. He asks, "Do you want to make a formal complaint?" I look at him and then at Justin, saying no. I can see him sweating. He can be harshly punished if I make a complaint. I sigh, knowing in my heart I can't do that. I am leaving tomorrow, so he will not be around Zander.

I ask, "Will his grandpa watch him?" I need to go for a run and clear my head. He chuckles and says, "Let me have him; Alicia will be so happy." I look at Justin. He had a hurt look on his face. I run to the river; I look into the trees to find an oversized shirt. The Pack always leaves clothes on tree branches. It is for when we change tearing our clothes.

I sit on a boulder by the lake. I hear a branch break, and I look back and see Justin's wolf (Duke). I ask what you want. Do you want to hurt me more? I do not know if I can take any more pain. He shifts and sits next to me. We sit in an awkward silence. Justin says, "I am sorry. I did not know you would feel me having sex." (Lie, we learn this when we are teens) "I am sorry I tricked you into giving me your virginity." (Lie number two) "I am sorry for running with Zander. I just wanted to get to know him." (Ok, I am not sure if that is a lie) "I am sorry I accused you of murder. I know I do not deserve your forgiveness, but you do deserve my sincere apologies." I look at him, not sure if I can trust his words. His eyes show me he is sincere.

I hear Luke call my name. I turn around and run into his arms. I ask, "What are you doing here?" Then we hear a loud growl from behind us. I look at him, saying, "You lost your right to be jealous." I grab Luke's hand and say, "Let us go." We walk back to mom's house, and I tell him everything that has happened here.

Then Louie walks in, and her wolf says, "MATE." They were staring into each other's eyes. I say, "Well, you are coming home with us, Louie." They were busy kissing, and I told them I would give them some privacy. I yell to them, "Stay out of my bedroom. Use mom's."

I walk into the house, and I see Luna playing with Zander. She asks, "How are you doing, baby?" I assure her I am fine. I told them that Louie had found her mate. She is going back with me; they smile. "I will call Alpha Red and get the transfer papers ready," says my adopted dad. I tell them I am scared to go back to mom's house right now, laughing.

Justin walks into the living room and asks me, "May I please spend time with Zander?" I tell him, "You can spend time but with your parents present. I do not trust you, Justin. Take it or leave it." He nods and walks over to Zander. I say if you need me, I will be at mom's house. I was praying I would not catch the new mates doing the nasty. Louie and Luke were fully mated by the time I made it back to the house. I can't wait to be an aunt to my best friend's babies.

Blue Moon Pack

I got my car packed, and we took some of Louie's stuff. The rest was loaded into Logins' truck. I started to cry when I said goodbye to Mark and Alicia. Justin walks out, handing me an envelope. I look confused. It is for you and Zander. He hugs me, and I feel all the sparks go through my body. I shove Justin away from me. Justin had a smile with hope in his eyes. I yell out, "OH HELL NO!" He still has the spark of hope in his eyes, and I say no, shaking my head. I ran to my car and left. Louie asks what happened. I told her I felt the sparks when he hugged me. Louie says If you both are rejected, it means your wolves have bonded. Louie asks what is in the envelope. I said I do not know. I am not sure if I want to know yet. It did not take long to get back home. We did not have to make stops. Louie would feed and change Zander's diapers.

We get back, and I hire a nanny. I now have a real estate office to run. The house mom left is rented out. I have five employees that also sell houses. I studied to get my real estate license so I could keep my business running effectively. I can sell homes also. I started taking online business classes to be more efficient.

The Mate Ball

This year it is the Blue Moon Pack's turn to throw the Mate Ball, the gathering for unmated wolves. Alpha's bring their daughters, hoping they get mated to other alphas. We are running around getting everything ready. I went and bought a new dress since I am one of the hostesses. It was a tight-fitting silver dress with a long slit on the side and silver heels.

I was checking on the caterers, bartenders, and decorations. The lights will be dimmed with twinkle lights around the ballroom. The tables had roses on them. The bars were set up in two different areas. There was a bar set up on the tables. There is nothing more romantic than roses. The band has already set up on stage. We also had set up outside with tables. There were twinkle lights with flowers on the tables. We set up buffet tables so they could eat when they were hungry. I had speakers set up outside with a dancing floor. I think it would be romantic if they could dance under the twinkling lights. They look like stars in the moonlight.

I finished up my work; then I got dressed. I go check on Zander and the nanny. The nanny was on the floor playing with him. I go downstairs, and guests are starting to arrive. I am welcoming everyone, and we had many packs joining us tonight.

I start to walk away, and I feel a hand on my elbow. I feel all the sparks going up my arm to my heart. I know that Justin just grabbed my arm without turning. I turn and ask, "What are you doing here?" He chuckles and says, "To look for my mate." I yank my arm away, telling him, "Happy hunting." I am still angry and hurt by the rejection. As I was walking away, I looked back and saw the hurt on his face. He kept following me all night, and it was getting annoying. As for my wolf Nyx, she loved it. She was making lewd remarks all night, things I am too embarrassed to mention. I do not have experience with men except for my one time with Justin.

I decided to go check on Zander. He was sleeping with the nanny and watching TV. I go to my room to use the bathroom. I walked out and got curious about the envelope Justin gave me. I opened it up, and there was a five-page letter. He poured his heart out to Zander and me. He put a cashier's check for $500,000. I get teary-eyed.

I hear a knock on the door, taking myself out of my thoughts. It was Justin. I walk out and say, "I must get back to the Ball." He asks, "Why did you come up here?" I look at him angrily, saying, "It is none of your business." He looks down, saying, "I regretted rejecting you the minute I walked out of your room." I said, "So, while you were regretting it, it was so easy to sleep with someone else. No, Justin, what you did is wrong and unforgivable. Please stop trying to make things hard for me," I tell him.

He growls softly as he blurts out, "I was drugged and was under a spell. That slut gave it to me right before I went into your room." I say, "Come on, stop making excuses for your behavior. Who killed the slut that I was accused of killing? It was the witch, Mary. She promised she would join the Pack. Mary told her as soon as she was made Luna, she was going to make changes. What is it the witch wanted? The witch wanted her covenant to be accepted back into the Pack. My grandfather ran them out when they killed my grandmother. She wanted to run the Pack as Luna. Mary asked for a love spell because I always turned down her advances. They did not expect me to find my mate, so the spell only worked for a while. The spell broke the day you were leaving. My wolf was able to take the drugs out of my system. The witch we have as a friend of the Pack helped me."

I could not understand what he was telling me. I say, "So I should just trust what you are saying? I do not trust you, to be honest," I say. He says, "Ask mom and dad, and they will tell you. They caught the witch when your mom was poisoned. She was the one that weakened your mom. She was poisoned by a rogue. Then the witch magnified the poison with magic. She made it to guarantee her death. Many feared your mom. She was a fierce fighter and an expert at war strategies. They had to use magic to kill her; they would not be able to beat her fighting without cheating." I was holding tears back for my mother. I decided to walk away from him.

I walk toward the party with Justin following me like a lost pup. He kept following me the whole night. My dad and Alpha Red were laughing and making jokes about him. Alpha Red tells me, "Mark him," and tells him he must earn the right to mark you. Place some rules, no touching, no hugging, and no sex until he proves himself. I hear my wolf Nyx in my head being a horny corndog. My human side just wants to kick his ass. I know it is going to be hard. Your wolves have not rejected each other. They are bonded to each other. I tell Alpha Red I do not trust him. Alpha Red says, "He was under a spell, little warrior. You are a woman; make him earn you and Zander. A woman can control a man if done right. Anyway, if you mark him first, you are the dominant one in the relationship. That is why we men mark women first. We are selfish animals in that way." I gasp, saying, "And you are admitting it to me?" He chuckles, saying, "If you repeat it, I will deny it. No man wants his secrets out there."

The Next Morning

After the Ball, Alpha Red gave permission for Justin to stay the night. He was on the same floor as us. I could smell his scent near, which was driving Nyx crazy. Okay, me too, but I will not let him know that. The next morning, Zander and I went to breakfast. There was Justin watching me carry Zander into the dining hall. I grabbed a plate for Zander and I. Just my luck. The only empty seat was in front of Justin. I was ignoring him, eating and feeding Zander.

Suddenly, Zander grabs a pancake and throws it across the table. The pancake lands smack in the middle of Justin's face. We all started laughing, including Justin. Zander is laughing the whole time, then gets another pancake when Justin looks away. This time it hit his cheek and ear, which were full of syrup. Justin laughs and says, "I need a second shower," while laughing. Zander starts eating his eggs and bacon. I guess his hunger got the best of him. Justin says, "Can I please hold him?" I say, "Hell no, you might try and steal him again. Your dad had to command you to give him back the last time." We hear growls all around the table. Justin says, "Zander has a lot of protection. Please, I will not move from the table," he is pleading with me. I see dad and Red giving me a warning glare. I let out a small growl. I reluctantly hand him Zander.

Justin had Zander giggling the whole time. I finish eating and say, "Give Zander back. He needs a bath." He says, "Please can I help?" I look at dad and Alpha Red; they nod yes. I am growling softly, telling him to follow me. I hate being an adult but still do as told by her dads. He is still holding Zander, making him laugh. We get to the nursery, and I am getting the water ready. He undresses Zander and puts him in the tub. I gave him a washcloth and baby soap. I watch as Justin gives him a bath. We dress him, and I take him to my room and place him in the playpen. He is playing with his toys and making his gibberish sounds. Justin sits on the bed, watching him.

He finally says, "Demi, please come home. Please give me a chance to be your mate again. I will start with dates, movie nights, and do whatever you want." I ask him, "Will you let me mark you first and do the dating stuff? Then, when I get to trust you again, I will let you mark me." Justin gives me a weird look and says okay. I have some conditions: No mating, no kissing, no hugging. Only when I feel safe again with you, then and only then, will I let you mark me. My mark will let the other she-wolves know you are taken.

My two dads want a discussion with you too. Do you accept these conditions? He does not even think about it and says yes. Justin says, "I will do it and let you do anything to me you want. I just want a second chance." I look at him, not sure if I should, but my wolf is begging me. I tell my wolf fine, but if he screws up, then we kick his ass. "Deal," my wolf says with a smile. She is happy she got what she wanted.

"Let me call dad so they can have your room ready," says Justin. "Dad wants to know if he can set up a nursery, or will he sleep in your room?" I say, "You can have a nursery set up for him, but he is sleeping in my room for now." Justin says, "Dad wants to talk to you." I got the phone, and Alpha Mark asked me, "Did he force you?" I said no, and he asked me to give him a chance. Our wolves are bonded. I told Mark I had some conditions. "I am going to mark him while we date." I hear him laugh loudly and say, "You are marking him, little one. I have to hand it to you. Little one, you are a smart cookie. I will send a van for your things. Start packing," he tells me.

I asked him, "Are you ready?" He says yes, and I ask, "Are you sure?" He says yes and shows me the inside of his neck. I sit on his lap with my legs straddling him. He smiles and says, "I like this." I roll my eyes, saying, "This is to get better access to your neck. Remember, I am not too tall." I trail kisses on his neck then I hear a moan. I found his sweet spot to mark. My wolf licks the area hearing another moan. Nyx pulls out her teeth and bites him. After a few seconds, Nyx lets go, licking the area. We werewolves can heal our mate's cuts with our saliva. Then I heard Nyx say, "Let me jump him now, please." I tell her, "Shut it, horny corndog. He must earn it." I am talking with him, and he closes his eyes while letting a soft moan out. That jerk was getting a hard-on. I gasped and jumped out of his lap. Nyx says, "Please," I ignore my wolf. Justin clears his throat realizing his wolf was putting sex thoughts in his head. He says, "Sorry, my wolf got carried away."

Justin says, "I need to head home. When will you arrive?" I said tomorrow night. I have packing to do and load up the van your dad is sending me. I remind him, "Stop by Alpha Red's office before you leave." He nods and suddenly looks terrified. I chuckle and say, "Good luck. You have two dads to deal with. Red is the meaner one of the two when it comes to me." I am happy knowing he is going to get an ear full. Maybe he should. He is going to get threatened with death.

Red Moon Pack

I have arrived at the Red Moon Pack, and Mark and Alicia are waiting for me. They hug me, then take Zander from my arms, and he keeps giggling with them. They say, "Come on, Justin will show you to Zander's and your room." Justin walks next to me with a smile. I tell him, "You seem happy." He says, "I have my mate and my son home where they belong. Demi, I know I have a lot of work to do. I promise you will not regret giving me a second chance."

I ask, "When I was away, have you been with other women?" He clears his throat and says, "I must be honest with you. Three weeks before your mom was poisoned, I slept with two women. They were nothing serious, and I made sure I told them that. They were one-night stands and did not mean anything to me. When I saw you with Zander, it was when I felt the bond reconnect by a thread. I never touched or desired another woman.

Duke also threatened if I cheated out bond again, he would kill the woman. The bond was activated again, and you would have felt it if I did. I hope I do not have problems with these women," I tell him.

I say, "Come on, I am hungry. I need to feed our son before he gets cranky." I walk into the kitchen and decide to make mac and cheese, saying, "Zander loves mac and cheese." I put Zander in his highchair while I start cooking. Justin says, "Let me get a bib for him," as he walks out of the kitchen.

A woman walks into the kitchen and says, "Justin will never be faithful. You will never make him change his ways by being here. I slept with him, and he is mine." I laugh and say, "You know I marked Justin. He will not cheat even if he tries; I will know." Justin walks in and says, "Lena, I made it perfectly clear we had a one-night stand. Lena, you agreed that you understood." (Lena grew up with us, and she became the pack slut. This is how she makes her money. The Alpha says it is her choice as long as she does it in town. This was not allowed on pack territory, which is a gray line since the town belongs to the Pack.) She says, "I am pregnant, and our baby will be Alpha." I burst out laughing; she is an omega. I link the doctor to send a pregnancy test to the kitchen. I tell her, "Follow the doctor to the nearest bathroom." She refuses, and I say, "I knew you were a liar. I suggest you leave us, or my wolf is going to kick your ass." She nods with tears in her eyes, saying, "But I love you, Justin." I say, "He is Alpha Justin to you. Try and remember that." He says, "No, you love that I am an Alpha, and you want to be Luna. I already have a mate that is going to be mine and the Pack's Luna." I wave bye to her, and she runs out of the back door, hopefully going home.

I hear "mommy," and I stop and smile, hearing Zander's first word. Justin then tells

Zander, "Say daddy," stretching out the word "daddy." Zander looks at him and says, "Mommy." I crack up laughing when Alpha Mark walks in, asking, "What is funny?" I say, "Watch," and Zander giggles and says, "Mommy." I point to Justin discreetly, and we see him pouting. Alpha Mark bursts out laughing, saying, "Son, all babies say mommy first. They are the main caregivers; we are usually busy working with the Pack. Besides, all boys become momma's boys, just like you still are."

The next morning, I get dressed for work and walk to the kitchen to make coffee. I tell Mark I have some errands to run and need to go into the office. I ask him if he wants to babysit, and he can also get help from the nanny who watches TV in Zander's room while he is sleeping. He says, "No problem," and then I hear Justin say, "Can I be your driver today?" I look at him, thinking about it, and then say, "Why not? I did say I would give him a chance. I need to get my purse and computer bag. Meet me at the door," I tell him. I pack my bag, making sure I have all the papers and my laptop. I have been doing an audit of my realty company.

When I walk into the foyer of our mansion, I see Justin talking to his father. Justin is hugging our son, and Zander is giggling. Justin is glowing with happiness, and he has been a perfect gentleman. I am surprised at how much he has grown up in the past year.

I say, "Ready?" He jumps, not realizing I was in the foyer. He had always sensed me before I entered a room, but I guess since he was busy with the baby, he was off guard. Justin is humming to the radio with a huge goofy smile on his face. I watch Justin drive with a goofy smile on his face. Suddenly, without warning, he bursts out singing. I laugh even louder because he sounds like a hyena in heat. We are at a red light, and the girls next to us burst out laughing at him. Still, he is unaffected; he is in such a good mood. He sings all the way to the bank. I don't know how my ears are not bleeding yet.

The Thief

I have arrived at the Red Moon Pack, and Mark and Alicia are waiting for me. They hug me, then take Zander from my arms, and he keeps giggling with them. They say, "Come on, Justin will show you to Zander's and your room." Justin walks next to me with a smile. I tell him, "You seem happy." He says, "I have my mate and my son home where they belong. Demi, I know I have a lot of work to do. I promise you will not regret giving me a second chance."

I ask, "When I was away, have you been with other women?" He clears his throat and says, "I must be honest with you. Three weeks before your mom was poisoned, I slept with two women. They were nothing serious, and I made sure I told them that. They were one-night stands and did not mean anything to me. When I saw you with Zander, it was when I felt the bond reconnect by a thread. I never touched or desired another woman.

Duke also threatened if I cheated out bond again, he would kill the woman. The bond was activated again, and you would have felt it if I did. I hope I do not have problems with these women," I tell him.

I say, "Come on, I am hungry. I need to feed our son before he gets cranky." I walk into the kitchen and decide to make mac and cheese, saying, "Zander loves mac and cheese." I put Zander in his highchair while I start cooking. Justin says, "Let me get a bib for him," as he walks out of the kitchen.

A woman walks into the kitchen and says, "Justin will never be faithful. You will never make him change his ways by being here. I slept with him, and he is mine." I laugh and say, "You know I marked Justin. He will not cheat even if he tries; I will know." Justin walks in and says, "Lena, I made it perfectly clear we had a one-night stand. Lena, you agreed that you understood." (Lena grew up with us, and she became the pack slut. This is how she makes her money. The Alpha says it is her choice as long as she does it in town. This was not allowed on pack territory, which is a gray line since the town belongs to the Pack.) She says, "I am pregnant, and our baby will be Alpha."

I burst out laughing; she is an omega. I link the doctor to send a pregnancy test to the kitchen. I tell her, "Follow the doctor to the nearest bathroom." She refuses, and I say, "I knew you were a liar. I suggest you leave us, or my wolf is going to kick your ass." She nods with tears in her eyes, saying, "But I love you, Justin." I say, "He is Alpha Justin to you. Try and remember that." He says, "No, you love that I am an Alpha, and you want to be Luna. I already have a mate that is going to be mine and the Pack's Luna." I wave bye to her, and she runs out of the back door, hopefully going home.

I hear "Mommy," and I stop and smile, hearing Zander's first word. Justin then tells Zander, "Say daddy," stretching out the word "daddy." Zander looks at him and says, "Mommy." I crack up laughing when Alpha Mark walks in, asking, "What is funny?" I say, "Watch," and Zander giggles and says, "Mommy." I point to Justin discreetly, and we see him pouting. Alpha Mark bursts out laughing, saying, "Son, all babies say mommy first. They are the main caregivers; we are usually busy working with the Pack. Besides, all boys become momma's boys, just like you still are."

The next morning, I get dressed for work and walk to the kitchen to make coffee. I tell Mark I have some errands to run and need to go into the office. I ask him if he wants to babysit, and he can also get help from the nanny who watches TV in Zander's room while he is sleeping. He says, "No problem," and then I hear Justin say, "Can I be your driver today?" I look at him, thinking about it, and then say, "Why not? I did say I would give him a chance. I need to get my purse and computer bag; meet me at the door," I tell him. I pack my bag, making sure I have all the papers and my laptop. I have been doing an audit of my realty company.

When I walk into the foyer of our mansion, I see Justin talking to his father. Justin is hugging our son, and Zander is giggling. Justin is glowing with happiness, and he has been a perfect gentleman. I am surprised at how much he has grown up in the past year.

I say, "Ready?" He jumps, not realizing I was in the foyer. He had always sensed me before I entered a room, but I guess since he was busy with the baby, he was off guard. Justin is humming to the radio with a huge goofy smile on his face. I watch Justin drive with a goofy smile on his face. Suddenly, without warning, he bursts out singing. I laugh even louder because he sounds like a hyena in heat. We are at a red light, and the girls next to us burst out laughing at him. Still, he is unaffected; he is in such a good mood. He sings all the way to the bank. I don't know how my ears are not bleeding yet.

When we walk into the bank, it looks empty. I go to the teller and deposit the check Justin had given me. I talk to the teller and tell her I need to talk to Mrs. Cooper. We are asked to wait in the lobby. It is set up with two couches and two chairs. It has an area rug in the middle with a vase of fake flowers on a coffee table. The chairs we are sitting in are uncomfortable.

The accounts manager is taking her sweet time, and I am getting impatient. A woman walks up to us and says, "Good morning. I am Mrs. Cooper. Miss Dennison, please follow me into my office." We walk down a hall towards the back of the bank. We walk into a small office with a large desk. She asks us to sit in the chairs in front of her desk. She asks me to sign some forms before she can hand me the documents I need. I had to give her a copy of the will along with two forms of identification.

She has printed out all the copies of deposits and check activity of my accounts. I have a nagging feeling someone has been stealing money from the company. As I wait for the paperwork, I look at Justin and say, "Stop staring." I say, "Just spit it out, tell me what is on your mind." He smiles and says, "I am just admiring the view." I blush and say, "You are making me nervous, so, cut it out."

The manager walks in, saying, "Here is all the documentation. These are the wire transfers that have been made." I ask, "What wire transfers?" She explains all the wire transfers one of my employees made to an account out of the country. I say, "Call me if they try to make another wire." She gives me a friendly smile, agreeing to call me. I am looking over all the reports and put them in my computer bag.

She says, "Now that you are the owner of the company and bank accounts, I keep the authorized persons. Do you want to change any account users? Mrs. Cooper asks?" I say, "Yes, only Justin Thomas and I are allowed to any of my accounts." She asks Justin for his two forms of identification and has him sign a paper.

On the way to the office, Justin asks, "Do you know who is embezzling money?" I do, but I want more evidence to make sure I nail her to the wall. When I get to the office, I see the bookkeeper is missing. I walk to my office, and the manager comes in. I look at her, and she hands me her reports for the last three months. I had called her in advance and told them I wanted everyone's reports.

I ask her, "Where is Molly?" Molly Miller is the bookkeeper of the company. She is in charge of the books and the money part of the sales. She says she did not show up to work today. I tried to call her, and she was not answering. I tell her, "Can you bring me her financial papers from her desk?" Molly is the bookkeeper that mom had trusted for many years. I think since I am so young, she thought she could do as she pleased. I have seen some discrepancies, so I have been investigating my company's financials. I noticed it after mom died. Molly took advantage of me being grief-stricken for my mother. I believe it might be my fault for not paying attention.

I turn on my computer, and the numbers are not adding up. I look at the bank statements and see a wire going out today. I call the bank not to send the transfer and to stall. I tell Justin to get some warriors to pick up Molly Miller from the bank. We have pack members that are policemen. "Hurry before she leaves the bank, have them bring her here," I say. I keep checking all the deposits and what comes in.

I was checking on houses that were sold, and my rental house was rented out. I noticed my grandmother's house was sold already and was pending inspections. The sale is not final yet because she needed my signature. I go to the door and say semi-loudly, "Who sold the house on Lexington Street?" The manager says, "Molly, she said you told her to." I start to make a fist, and my claws are starting to extend. Justin pulls me into his chest. He reminds me that the office manager is human. I begin to calm down and pull away from Justin. I sit back in my chair; I ask Justin to talk to Jenny (she is a realtor mom hired) about my grandmother's furniture and knick-knacks. He nods as I start to work on my books. I have sent Jenny to show a couple of houses. I want us to have privacy when Molly arrives.

When she arrives, Molly sees me and gulps. Molly lost all her color from her face. I motion for her to sit, and I wait for Justin. He mind-links me and says, "Everything is in a storage facility." I looked at Molly and asked her if she was planning a trip. She looks down and whispers yes. I ask, "Why are you stealing from me? If you needed money, I would have helped you. Why sell my grandmother's house from under me?" She gulps, saying that was your grandmother's.

Molly, you being a wolf, you do know that you will be punished, right? She starts to cry, and I tell her to stop crying. I say, "Tell me about the house you sold." She then told me it was not completed since she did not have my signature. I put it on my desk in a red folder. I ask Justin, "Will you be a dear and get me the red folder?" I open it up and call the buyer. I tell him the property is not for sale. I told him the seller changed their mind and that he would get his deposit back. I will leave the check-up in front with a little extra for his time," I tell him. "If he still wants to buy a house, we can have another agent help you," I inform him. I then tell him to call the office manager to be waiting for his call. I ask the office manager to help find me a bookkeeper to interview. Make sure to run background checks before setting up appointments.

I close my office and have the warrior wait outside my door. I tell her to transfer the money back to my account now. I handed her a laptop, and Justin was watching her. I ask, "All done?" He nods. I pick up the phone and call Alpha Mark. I want to formally make a complaint about theft. Can you please fax me the papers to sign? "Two guards are taking her in now," I tell Mark. I tell the warriors to take her to the cells to wait for judgment. I then say, "No one touches her until then," they say, "Yes, Luna." Justin pulls his chair close and says, "How did you find the discrepancies so fast?" I told him I had a feeling already and did the work at home. I am a math whiz, remember?

I tell Justin, "Now that the house is empty, let us see what repairs are needed." I grab all the paperwork I need and grab a laptop from a drawer. I say, "I am going to work from home. Call me if you need me." The manager says, "Yes, ma'am, I will have the list of applicants for you tomorrow." I say, "Ok, thank you, please do the background checks too, please?" I told her about the man coming tomorrow for the check I gave her. I tell her, "Will you personally take care of him? Try and see if he wants to see a different house. There is a house on Jarrad St. that is similar to my grandma's house."

Gramma's house

When we got there, I noticed that it needed a new roof and landscaping. The interior needed new paint and shutters. Justin pulls out a clipboard from his truck and says, "You also need new windows. I recommend double pane for saving energy." I decided I wanted both bathrooms gutted and redone. The kitchen, I also wanted the gutted and remodeled. I want a huge kitchen island and natural wood cabinets with black metal handles. I told him I wanted the garage closed and added to the house; I wanted a huge living room and dining room. I want it all in an open concept. I want the carpet out of the whole house; I want hardwood floors and the walls a soft light grey.

We walk out the back door, and I tell him I want a screened-in deck the width of the house and eight feet out. I want it to face a garden with a walkway leading into the woods. I look at Justin, and he is smiling at me. I say, "What?" He says,

"You have great ideas here." He asks, "Can we live here when you accept me fully?" I say, "I thought you had to live in the pack house." He tells me, "I have to work there, but I can live near the pack house. This house is a ten-minute drive and a minute in wolf form." I smile and say, "We will see; I still have to learn to trust you."

Justin says, "Let me have this project." I hand him my check, saying, "This is my budget." He says, "No, you are my mate, so please let me do this for you." I say, "On one condition." He says, "Ok, shoot." I say, "If for any reason you mess up, and I reject you, I can sue you for the build." He frowns and says, "You will trust me again." I say, "Deal or no deal." He says, "Fine, yes, deal." Justin owns a construction company that hires only werewolves.

Trespassers

The next day, we met with the contractors, and they found a secret room with rogues. I followed the contractor, and there was a woman with a child. I asked, "What are you doing here?" The woman had her face down and said, "I am sorry. We needed shelter last night; I noticed it was empty. It started to rain, and I did not want Amber to get sick. I do not mean any disrespect; we were just passing through. Please just let us go. I promise we will not come back."

I asked, "What are your names?" The woman replied, "I am Fina Lotus, and this is Amber Lotus. Amber is my niece; her parents are dead." I asked them to stay and eat something. She nodded, and I got my phone and ordered pizzas. I asked her why she left her Pack. She told me that her old Alpha had killed Amber's parents. She escaped to save Amber. The Alpha was going to kill her too. She said that the Alpha was in love with her sister-in-law. She never loved him, and when she found her mate, he got obsessed. He was always making passes at her, but you know how mates are. She would not tell her mate. Then last week, the Alpha was forcing himself on Amber's mom. Her mate tried to protect her, but the Alpha was a dirty fighter. The Alpha killed them both and then was looking for Amber. I quickly packed my clothes and ran away with Amber.

I went outside and called Mark. He drove over, and he talked to her in private. Mark felt their pain and made them pack members. He took them and assigned them a pack cottage.

After three months, the house was finally finished, and I was going to see what Justin did to it. It really looked beautiful and homey. I got modern furniture but kept what I liked from Grandma's. The whole house looked pretty; there was a patio and a small garden in the back, just like I wanted. I decided to take Justin out for dinner to thank him. We went for pasta at a charming little Italian restaurant. We had a fun time, then went home. I checked on Zander and then went to bed.

Attempted Kidnapping

I was at my grandma's house with the nanny, Zander, Amber, and a warrior (aka Freddy). Freddy was my mom's right hand. I was out back cutting flowers to arrange them in a vase when four rogues came out of the woods. We were under attack from four rogues who wanted to kidnap me. One of them grabbed me and was about to put me over his shoulder when Freddy knocked him down. I jumped up and got ready to fight. Another rogue came at me, and I fought him off. Nyx came forward and broke his neck. That was a quick fight. I grabbed the kids and put them in the secret room.

Freddy fought the first rogue. He clawed his stomach, and they shifted into their wolf forms. I saw the wolves rolling around, clawing and biting each other. I heard a growl, and Freddy tore the rogue's throat out. One of the wolves was still looking for me. I found him in my living room. I took off running out the back door. He jumped me, and I fell to the ground. I quickly got up and got ready to fight. I shifted into my wolf form, which was smaller than his. He had to be a high-status wolf. I kept evading his attacks. Nyx said, "He is pissing me off." When he jumped again, Nyx caught his neck and tore out his throat. I looked at Freddy, and I saw him tear the throat out of the final rogue.

Justin came running in wolf form. He had sensed that I was distressed. Then Freddy told Justin, "I am not losing Warrior Dennison's daughter. I promised her I would take care of her." He cut his hand and grabbed my hand, combining our blood. He said, "I, Freddy Brown, am making a blood oath to die protecting Demetria Dennison, my future Luna." Power of some sort surged through my veins, stopping at my heart. Then he poked Zander's little finger and made the same oath. I was in shock, for I never saw that coming. I looked at Justin, completely confused. Justin pulled me aside and told me, "Freddy was there when your mom was attacked. He tried defending her, but the witch said a chant and froze him. He saw them give your mom several injections. They beat your mom when she was on the ground, unable to move. When they left, he promised your mom he would take care of you and Zander. This is the reason he is assigned to you." I just stood there because I only knew she was weakened and poisoned. I had no idea how much she was tortured.

The Date

The following week, Justin asked me if I wanted to go for dinner and dance after. I agreed, and after work, I went to buy a dress for the occasion. I found a snug red dress that went down to my thighs and bought red heels to match. When I walked down the stairs, I saw Justin's eyes turn black with lust. I told him to calm down and reminded him it was just dinner and dancing. He gulped and said, "I know, baby girl, you look so sexy in that dress." I teased him, saying, "I can go change if you like." He grabbed my hand, saying, "Hell no, if I cannot touch you, at least I can look at my eye candy." I blushed at his comment, and we walked out holding hands.

He took me to a fancy restaurant, and we talked about everything and anything. Then we went to the Wolf's Den for dancing (a wolf-owned club). Justin had a table reserved for us with champagne. Whenever Justin would go to the bathroom, men would come and ask me to dance. I would decline, of course, but it would sometimes lead to growls and tensions due to the mate bond. He almost got into a fight with one werewolf. I would just laugh it off and say, "Come on, let us dance." We danced until the last call. When we got home, he walked me to my room, and we kissed. It was hard to fight the mate bond. I told him I would meet him for breakfast.

I changed into my pajamas, and then I heard Zander start to cry. I went to his room, picked him up, and brought him to my room. I put him in bed with me, propping pillows on the other side of him. He fell asleep right away. I started dreaming that someone was trying to steal Zander. I started to scream for them to give him back. Then I felt someone holding my arms and heard Zander crying. I woke up and saw Justin holding my hands. He asked, "Are you okay now?" I nodded, and he let me go so he could go pick up Zander. I got up and went to wash my face. When I came back, Zander was asleep again. Justin asked me what I had been dreaming about, and I said someone had taken Zander from us. I was trying to get him back, but the more I tried, the further he got away from me. He told me to scoot over and held me until I fell asleep again.

The next morning, I woke up and was alone in bed. I got up, took a shower, and went downstairs. Justin had Zander in a highchair, making breakfast. I said good morning, and Zander giggled, saying, "Mommy." I kissed his forehead and sat on the island. I asked why he didn't wake me up, and Justin said, "I was going to take you breakfast in bed, but you jumped the gun." We ate, and I told him I needed to go to the office. He offered to help and suggested using his truck to fit the playpen. He also mentioned that I needed a bookkeeper to replace Molly. I smiled and said, "Okay, be ready in an hour."

When we got to the office, I rearranged my office to fit the playpen in the corner. I got all my paperwork done, and Justin brought the books up to date. I asked one of the girls to take everyone's deli order for lunch. I have three employees who are realtors, and I told them to stay in the office today to catch up on paperwork. I planned to audit everyone today.

I told Justin to use the office card from the petty cash. He said, "Yes, ma'am." I smiled and said, "You never had a female boss before, have you?" He replied, "Nope, but trust me, I am not complaining." Then he whispered, "But now that I do, it's a turn-on." I blushed again and walked away. When I looked over my shoulder, I saw him looking at me. I added a little sway to my hips, and I heard a low growl in my head. I mind-linked him and said, "Stop looking at my ass." He laughed out loud, and I mind linked back, "Busted." My manager, who is human, looked at Justin, laughing out loud. He looked at her and said, "Cat videos." She just smiled and replied, "You are not allowed to use company computers to watch videos." I mind-linked him again, "You can be punished for breaking my rules." His mind linked back, "Nyx would love that." I shook my head and blushed at him. I mind-linked him again, saying, "I know Nyx is a slut. We have been flirting like crazy lately. I know it is all this sexual frustration we are feeling. I have been thinking of completely solidifying our bond."

My Heat

We had a movie night in Justin's room. We were watching a movie while I sat on his lap. Justin started kissing me passionately, so much so that we had to stop to catch our breath. He turns me around where I am straddling him. I was all flushed and told him we needed to stop. I hear Nyx growl in my head with frustration. He looks at me, saying, "I am sorry. It is hard for me to keep my hands off you." I said, "It is okay," and I told him I was going to check on Zander and go to bed. We kiss again, and I get off his lap. He comes with me to check on Zander and then pushes me to the wall, kissing me.

I tell him, "Please stop. I am not ready." He backs away, and I go to my room. I take a cold shower and get into bed. Nyx says, "Are you sure you are not ready?" I told her, "I do not know. I am scared to move on." Nyx says, "We need to give him a chance. He has proven he loves us and is sincere with us." I say, "I know; I am thinking of letting him mark me."

I woke up at 3 a.m.. I had the worst headache. I started to burn and feel pain like no other. I mind linking Justin, telling him I feel sick. I heard the door open, and he ran in. He says, "What is wrong, baby girl?" Then I hear Nyx say, "We are in heat; she needs your help." We go in heat at least twice a year; then our period comes after. It only comes if we are not pregnant. The heat lasts three days, and the period two days. We go in heat to procreate. It is to ensure the Pack keeps growing.

We hear howling and growling. I see Justin mind-linking, then I hear whimpering. Nyx repeats, "Please, Justin, help me, babe." He says, "No, you will hate me afterward." Nyx reassures him, "Please, I promise I will not. We were already going to give in tomorrow. I feel like a wonton begging for sex. That crazy, horny wolf I have." I tell Nyx, "I never agreed to this." She is freaking ignoring me. "Please help her. She needs you. What the hell, Nyx!" She tells me to shut it and let me enjoy our mate.

Justin starts kissing me and slowly undressing me. He kisses my neck, working his way to my hardened nipples. He has his mouth on one while his other hand gives my other breast attention. He starts working his way down my belly with small kisses. He makes his way down to my heart. I feel him sucking on my nub. He starts to insert his finger into me. It is taking me over the top. I am ready to explode all over his finger. He adds another finger, and I explode onto his fingers. He smiles and starts to enter me. He is slowly entering to tease me. He starts picking up the speed, and my back arches, wanting him all. We were locked in my room for three days. Justin called work and told them I was sick. Justin would get food and water when I fell asleep. He took care of me during my heat. When the three days were over, Justin asked, "Can I mark you?" I told him yes, and I moved into his room. Mark gave us the Pack when we became full mates. We set the wedding and Luna Ceremony for two months. I wanted to make it special. I wanted to buy a dress for the occasion.

The Alpha and Luna Ceremony

Alicia and I are dress-shopping for the Luna ceremony. We walk into the bridal shop. I found out I am two months pregnant. We decided to buy a ballroom dress. I chose a satin white one-shoulder dress with crystal crystals and pearls on the whole top. It had a mini skirt with a sheer white skirt over it. The sheer skirt on the front fell below my knee, and the back was five inches below the knee. I bought a pair of white low heels; I bought crystals and pearls to put in my hair.

It is a bittersweet moment for me; my mom should be here with me. The Luna ceremony is also a wedding between wolves. My dad and Alpha Red will be here for me. Luke and Louie are joining me also. I cannot have this day without my two best friends. Justin is walking on cloud nine; he cannot wait for our wedding to be official. We ordered a cake and a band for music. The cooks are making a special dinner for us.

The day is here, and everyone is running around like crazy. The nanny is chasing Zander around; he is two years old already. I am in my room with Alicia and Louie. Alicia hired professionals to do our hair and makeup. I was not allowed to stay with Justin last night. So, I had trouble falling asleep last night. I ended up sleeping late. I ate breakfast in my room. Alicia did not want me to see Justin. It is time now, and I hear Zander crying in the hall. I open the door. He is standing at the door and saying, "I want mommy." I laugh and tell him to come on in. The nanny comes running around the corner with his clothes. I smile and say, "Come in. Is he giving you a tough time?" She smiles and nods at me. "This boy of yours should be a cheetah with the speed he has," the nanny jokes.

It is time to go down, and dad walks me down. I get to the stairs of the stage, and I see Justin's hand being cut. His dad then cuts his and

Justin's hand. They hold their hands in the air. Alpha Mark asks, "Justin Thomas, as Alpha, do you promise to care for and protect the Red Moon Pack? Do you promise to lead with a firm hand but with dignity? Do you promise to help the Pack to prosper and have harmony?" He says yes, then I, Alpha Mark Thomas give you the Red Moon Pack. We hear the Pack howling, whistling, and clapping for Justin. Then Mark and Alicia go sit in their chairs on stage.

Then Justin says, "I call my mate and future Luna, Demetria Dennison, to come onto the stage." I walk out, and his eyes bulge out, and he smiles from ear to ear. I walk to him, and the minister gets us married. Then Justin says, "As Alpha of the Red Moon Pack, I present my mate, my wife." He pulls out the ceremony knife, he says, "Now for the Luna oath." We heard someone say, "I challenge Demetria Dennison Thomas for Luna of the Red Moon Pack." There were growls of disapproval throughout the crowd. Alicia stands and says, "Demetria is pregnant with the future heir. The wolf law says if the future Luna is pregnant, she can ask for a warrior to fight for her. Is there a warrior willing to fight for her?" the Luna asks. To my amazement, every warrior from Blue Moon and Red Moon Pack stands. I hear throughout the clearing saying, "I will accept the challenge for my future, Luna." I was in tears seeing so many people willing to fight for me. I look at Justin and ask what do I do? He says wolf law states if every female wolf warrior is willing to fight, the challenge is forfeited. In this case, it is two packs.

Suddenly, a warrior from the Blue Moon stands up. She says, "I will fight anyway." This warrior is six feet tall and is built like a linebacker. The challenger gulps and knows she cannot take it back. The challenger says she is not from our Pack. Then her twin jumps in the ring and says,

"But I am. Just to let the challenger know, Demi's mom Donna, trained me." The challenger gets in the ring and regrets it. This warrior automatically punches her in the face. She sways and gets into a fight stance again. The challenger throws a punch, and the warrior catches her hand. She twists it, and you can hear the wrist break. She cries out in pain. Then the warrior does a roundhouse kick. She knocks her out. The warrior says, "Someone takes her to the infirmary. According to wolf law, she was demoted to omega and will never be able to advance." I then go through the Luna ceremony. I thanked every warrior for their support. I left the party early because I was tired. Everyone else partied late.

The Babies

Three months later, I woke up and went to take a shower. As I am walking downstairs, I feel a sharp pain. While opening a link for Justin, I scream out in pain. I whisper, "Justin, I need you. I am at the stairs." He comes looking for me, and then I take another step. Another contraction comes in full force, and I almost fall to my knees. I lose my footing and fall down some steps; everything goes black.

I can sense Justin picking me up and running to the infirmary. I wake up smelling sanitizers and hear a machine beeping. I see Justin lying next to me, and I notice my stomach is gone. I start to cry, and Justin wakes up. He asks, "Are you in pain?" I ask, "Where are my babies?" Then I hear crying. He walks to the bassinet at the foot of my bed. He picks up two baby girls and brings them to me. He says, "Calm down, baby girl. You fell down the stairs during labor. The doctor had to perform a cesarean; you hit your head hard. Baby girl, you were in a coma for a week; let me call the doctor."

Dad comes running in and tells me not to scare him anymore. I smile and say, "I promise not to fall down the stairs when pregnant." He starts laughing, and then Alpha Red comes in. He says, "Little one, you make beautiful babies." Louie comes in and scolds me for scaring her like that. I just smile, taking it all in. I have amazing people around me, and I feel the love they have for me. I would never change it for anything. Justin's mind links me and says, "What is going on in your head?" I mind linking him and saying, "I am just enjoying all the love around me." He asks, "Do you have any names?" I say yes, "Donna and Alicia after our moms. They were like sisters, and I know these sisters will love each other the same way." Alicia comes over, hugging me while crying, saying thank you, dear.

The King's Competition

The Wolf King wants to retire but has no heir, so he is holding an Alpha competition. When an Alpha wants to step down, it goes first to his heir. If there is no heir, then the Beta will take over. He was preparing to give the throne to his Beta. The day before his coronation was performed, he was found dead in his bed. There was an investigation performed, and the killer was Lady Gamma. She is in the cell waiting for her judgment. She believed that the gamma would be next in line for the king. The law states the Beta is next in line. If he can't or refuses the throne, an alpha will be appointed. The gamma asked to be moved to another pack after his mate was sentenced to death. The king approved but not until the competition was over. The gamma is devoted to the king and agrees. The king came up with the competition to have an alpha earn the right to be king.

He has invited Alphas from all over the world to join a competition. The Alpha must have an invitation from the king and council to compete. The judges will be the wolf council and, of course, the king. I am excited not to be king but to be the competition. The beast in alpha looks forward to showing off our strengths. It is in our blood to prove we are the best of the best.

We will compete for strength, knowledge, and integrity. If the Alpha has had charges against them, they will be disqualified. They must meet all requirements and be willing to compete fairly. Anyone caught cheating or behaving without honor will be disqualified.

The requirements:

1. Must have an invitation.
2. Have a mate to carry an heir.
3. No charges were given by the council or king.
4. Must have wolf law knowledge.

5. Show integrity with their Pack during the competition.
6. Have the strength to protect his or her Pack.
7. Have a strong Beta's loyalty to the Pack.
8. The ability to enforce wolf law fairly.
9. Put his Pack first before himself.

Demi is helping me pack my bag. I am going to miss my family. I will be separated from her for a week. I will not see her until Saturday morning. I fly out on Friday and stay in a hotel nearby. I am studying all the books I can find about wolf laws and what is expected from me. I am going to miss my babies when I leave them for twelve days. Freddy got special permission to go with Demi. It is due to the blood oath he made. I am feeling a lot of pressure right now. I know once I get there, I will feel more confident. The competition is on a mountain in Canada.

Justin's Competition

Alpha Red, Beta Andrew (Red's Beta), Beta Jim (Justin's Beta), and I arrive in Canada. We were taken to a hotel. In the morning, we will receive instructions on what to do.

After breakfast, we all receive a card with instructions. We are to leave our luggage in front of our rooms. We are to take what we need to hike up a mountain and go rock climbing. We were paired with our betas. I am guessing they want to see how well we work as a team. When we got to the top, I noticed we were the first to arrive. We were led to our rooms, and we were told to shower and relax. We would be called when dinner was ready. We heard as others made it up the mountain. At dinner, we were told of four teams being disqualified for cheating. We were given an itinerary for the days to come.

Day 1: Testing wolf laws and integrity / on paper

Day 2: Assessed the ability to know when lied to/in person and on paper.

Day 2: Testing on the ability to solve problems / on paper.

Day 3: Strength/weights

Day 3: Strength/weights

Day 4: Ability to fight.

Day 5: Ability to fight.

Day 6: Ability to fight.

Day 7: Luna testing on humanity/paper and in person

Day 8: Luna's fighting skill

Day 9: Luna's fighting skills.

Day 10: Interview with king and council (alone)

Day 11: The ability for an Alpha and Luna to work together in a conflict and what action to take.

Day 12: A new king will be announced, / Ceremony for the king and queen.

The testing and assessments are kept between the judges. We have no idea how we did, but it is a determination for final decisions. When we finally finish with testing, the weight competition begins.

The two men with the picked up the least amount of weight were sent home. The next day two more were sent from the weight challenge. We next have to prepare for the fighting challenges. The tournament is set up to fight until there are only two left. Those two then fight to be the best fighters in the werewolf community. This status is an honor to have.

We broke for dinner, and we were told our mates would be arriving tomorrow. We are ecstatic; it is hard being away from our mates for too long. It has been hell without Demi and my pups.

Luna's Arrival

When we arrived, we were waiting in a field for choppers to pick us up. They are going to take us to the top of the mountain. I am looking for Justin, dad, and Alpha Red. The men are standing around waiting for their mates. I see Justin and run up to him. Oh, Goddess, how much I miss him.

Luna's assessments are going to start in an hour. I shower and get dressed, wearing my jeans with a T-shirt. Justin told me to be ready for anything. I grab my combat boots; I want to be comfortable. The first part of the test is two hours long. As I am looking through the test, I think that this is all common sense. Thanks to the Goddess, I finally finished. We were led to the cafeteria for lunch. We will start again in two hours.

We needed to do our second part of the assessment. The next test was on wolf laws and punishment. We had to figure out the punishment for each crime. Should we have compassion or not? When we are finished, we are to go into another room.

In this room, we have a person who tells us the story of their crime. We had to figure out if any or all were lies. We were given a small notebook and wrote what we would do. We must figure out a punishment that is due or compassion. Then we go to dinner and have the rest of the night off. I feel a headache coming on.

The next day after breakfast, I walk over to the rings. The last fight is going on. I see it is Justin and Alpha Red. This will show who is a better fighter. A woman next to me asked who you think will win. I look at her. I do not know, but it must be hard for them to fight each other. She looks at me and says why do you think that? I say, one is my mate, and the other is like my second dad. The woman looks at me and says it must be hard for you too. They are matched on their fighting skill, then Justin throws him out of the ring with a kick. The referee acknowledged Justin as the winner. If you get thrown out of the ring, the fight is over. Justin gets out and goes and shakes Alpha Red's hand, saying good fight. I run to both and hug them tightly. I tell him tomorrow is my turn to fight. Justin is the winner of fighting skills.

I get in the ring, waiting for my opponent, and she never shows up, so I am the winner. I found out she did not know how to fight. Her mate knew my mom's reputation and would not let her in the ring.

When it was time for me to fight again, Luna was a tall, muscular woman. I am not going to lie. I was scared. Alpha Red tells me, little one, remember your mom's training. I hear my wolf say. We got this, just do not overthink it. She lands the first punch, and it hurts like hell. I get in a fighting stance again, and this time I block the next punch. I got a punch in and hit her nose. I do not know how I hit so high. Oh boy, this pissed her off. She hits my rib, and I hear bones crack. She smiles, and I sweep her feet. I land on her and have my knees on her arms. I keep punching until she taps out. I was going to shake her hand, and she hit it away.

I had a third fight after lunch. I jump into Justin's arms, and he asks me if my face hurts. I say, "Hell yeah." that Luna has power in her punch.

I say, "Let us go eat. I am starving."

An hour later, I had my final match. Not all Lunas knew how to fight. They got 4 points taken off for that. The Luna that did not show up for the fight got disqualified. The Luna could have shown up and tapped out; they take off 4 points. The final fight was a hard fight; we were perfectly matched, but my final blow knocked her out, and I was announced the winner.

The next test evaluated us on the ability to analyze the problem and correct it. If it was a crime that was committed, we had to work together for the punishment. Justin and I have always worked together, so this part we knew we had it in the bag.

A councilman asks, Luna Demetria, why do you have a warrior as a bodyguard? Freddy says, I mean no disrespect, but may I answer the question? Freddy was on one knee with his head bowed, and he was waiting for the answer. The king tells him to rise and says enlighten me. Her mother was my partner; she was also head of the warriors. We were attacked by some witches and poisoned to kill her slowly. I was frozen in place and was forced to watch. When they left, the spell was broken, and I promised to protect her daughter. Well, when I was on guard at her grandmother's house, four rogues tried to kidnap her. I was getting the bags out of the car when I heard the commotion. I ran, and she managed to kill one, and I killed three of them. I could not live with myself if they had succeeded, so I made a blood oath.

My Luna is loved by both Red Moon Pack and Blue Moon Pack. At her own Luna ceremony, she was pregnant and challenged by one warrior. By wolf law, she could appoint a warrior to fight for her. Well, all the females from both packs volunteered. So, you see, she is a great Luna, and I will not let anything happen to her. She is an asset to all the wolves in our Pack. I was in tears and went to give him a hug.

The king smiles and says that shows that you are a great leader. The king says, ok, everyone eats dinner, and the council. I will evaluate all the events of the ten days. Tomorrow morning, we will announce the new king.

We go to eat dinner, and an Alpha and his Luna come sit with us. The Luna goes, you think you're special just because you have a bodyguard? I say, no, I am fortunate that I have him. If that makes me special, then I will wear that hat with pride. She looks at me and throws her food at me.

Both Justin and Freddy stand up, and I put my hand up to stop them. I sigh and ask them, please sit. She is not worth it. I look directly into her eyes; I tell her it is sad that Luna has not learned to behave as an adult. I suggest you control your jealousy and leave me alone. She growls, and I growl louder, and she whimpers. I look around and see some alphas and their Luna bow. The king watched the whole situation from where he and the council were sitting. My food had coffee mixed with the food. Justin brings me a new tray. He sits me on his lap, and we start to feed each other.

We go back to our room, and I strip and get in the shower. Alpha Red comes to our room looking for me. When I get out of the shower, he tells me, little one, you sure have a lot of control. I would have lost control. I just smile, and I say I am going to take a nap. Call me when it is time. We heard an alarm go off, and we were under attack. I jumped up and put on my combat boots and my belt of weapons. Justin kisses me and says fight smart and be careful.

The rogues found out we were all here. They figured they'd kill all the alphas and get their packs. Kill the king, and you become the king of all werewolves.

I got out of my tent and started fighting. The Lunas that did not fight were ushered into one tent, so I decided to protect them. I was killing rogues, and Freddy found me. We fought as a team side by side.

The Alpha of the rogues says, "You're mine." I roll my eyes and say, "Whatever." I get into a fighting stance. He is rushing to me, and I jump out of the way. We started to fight, and we were blocking each other's hits. I found a weakness in his left leg. I swept his leg and then kicked his ribs when he was down. He grunts and jumps to his feet. He was letting his anger get the best of him. He throws a punch to the side, and I get hit on the back shoulder blade. He smiles, letting his guard down. I do a roundhouse kick, hitting him in the face. He rips my clothes with his claws. He was hoping it would shock me and put my guard down. It did the opposite; I was on high alert.

He threw a knife at me, and Freddy got in the way. The knife hit him in the chest. I got so angry that I got my knife and slit his throat while he was laughing evilly. Then Nyx comes forward and rips his head off. She growls over the Battle.

Everyone stops, and some of them even bow to me. She says, "Your Alpha is dead," and throws the head on the ground. "Now leave, or you will get the same." One of the rogues says, "We are stronger than you." Nyx throws a silver knife to his throat and asks, "Anyone else?" The rogues take off running away.

Justin comes over and gives me his shirt. I started to cry and said that the knife was for me. Freddy says, "Blood oath, my Luna," and smiles at me. I cry, and I tell Justin to help me take him to the medic. He will survive, but it will take longer to heal. They had silver, which slowed down our healing. I donate some blood since he lost a lot of it.

The next morning, we all have breakfast. An alpha comes up to me, asking, "Who taught you to fight?" I say, "My mother, Donna Dennison. She was the head warrior for the Red Moon Pack." He says, "I thought you looked so much like her. She was visiting a small town near my Pack. A couple of rogues caught me by surprise. They injected me with wolfsbane with a sedative. She beat them senselessly. She tied them up with silver and took me to my Pack. I owe your mother my life. When I saw you fighting in the ring, I recognized the moves." I am sorry for your loss, Luna. I smile and thank him for telling me a story about my mom.

We hear the bells and announcements for us to meet outside. We go sit in the chairs that were set up for us. The king and the council members are sitting on a stage.

The king stands, giving us his speech.

"Can we have Alpha Red and his Beta on stage? Can Alpha Justin, Alpha Demetria, Beta Ben, and Freddy please come to the stage? Yes, everyone, you heard right, Alpha Demetria killed an alpha and a beta. She absorbed their strength from them.

Alpha Demetria protected the Lunas that could not fight. Alpha Demetria and Freddy were the only ones that remembered the Lunas that could not fight. Alpha Demetria killed the Alpha

Rogue and his Beta last night. Freddy made a blood oath to protect Luna; he took a knife for her.

Three of the council members will be retiring. Alpha Red, Freddy, and Beta Andrew (my dad), we want you to take their place. We also want Alpha Demetria on the council. You can keep your packs but will also have meetings with council business.

Now, Alpha Justin, you will be our next Wolf King. Alpha Demetria, you will be our next Queen of the Wolves. It was a good tournament, and these two people succeeded beyond our imaginations. We even saw a conflict in which another Luna threw her food all over Alpha Demetria. Alpha Demetria composed herself with dignity. If it were any other person here, their claws would be out. Congratulations to all that competed and survived. Alpha Demetria, thank you for saving the Lunas; it would have weakened their mates.

I will talk in private to the future king and queen."

Homecoming

We make it home and call a pack mandatory meeting in one hour. When everyone arrives, Justin says, "We have several announcements. I am the new Wolf King, and Freddy is a new council member. Your Luna is now an Alpha, a council member, and the Wolf Queen. She killed an alpha and his Beta when rogues attacked our camp. The Royal Pack and Royal Guards will be arriving next week. The Royal Witches will transform the whole Pack to the palace. Curfew next Friday at 5:00 p.m. sharp. Anyone not here will stay behind. If you would like to transfer out, meet me in the morning to get the paperwork done."

My Final Story

I am the happiest wolf alive now. Zander is old enough to be king. He chose to go to college first and find his mate. He is already 24 years old and finally found his mate. She was a tourist from England.

My daughters found their mates right away. One is a Luna, and the other is her Beta. They got trained by the Royal Guards and me to fight. They got the best of two unique styles of fighting. They also marked their mates first. They did not trust their mates since they were man whores.

As for myself and Justin, we are still so in love. I sold my realtor company; I have my hands busy being a Queen. The word got out that the Queen beheaded an alpha. We have not had a rogue attack in many years. My dad was killed in a car accident a while back. Alpha Red is still considered like a dad to me. Mark and Alicia are also my parents. Freddy was killed protecting Zander. It was a great loss to my family. My girls were attached to him and took it hard.

My hardships have made me a better person and anything good in my life were memories made. Justin had grown up since the day he rejected me. Justin proved to me every day what unconditional love is. He is the greatest dad ever, and the girls learned to say "daddy" before "mommy." Imagine what that did for his ego.

The End

Printed in Great Britain
by Amazon

37372104R00069